Mighty Mimi

Mimi, the tiny Bichon, tells of her
journey from meek to mighty.

as told to

Margo Mayberry

designed and illustrated by

Phyllis Stewart

Copyright

Copyright 2011 by Margo Mayberry
Mighty Mimi Version 2 - 978-1460903025
ISBN-10: 1460903021
www.createspace.com

Cover Design, illustrations and layout by Phyllis Stewart
Phyllis can be contacted at pstewart0831@sbcglobal.net
Margo can be contacted at wheresduffybook@wowway.com

All proceeds from this book will go to help support the

Ohio Puppy Rescue

www.ohiopuppyrescue.com

Printed in the USA

Dedication

This book is dedicated to all the animals still trapped in puppy mills until the rescue groups can get to you. It is also dedicated to the human volunteers who work so hard to help animals find forever homes where they can live their lives in peace, safety, and happiness.

The foster families for the **Ohio Puppy Rescue** help the injured, abandoned, and rescued animals and this book's proceeds will be donated to that agency.

Introduction

Have you ever been afraid during a thunderstorm? Has some strange dog scared you when you walked past it? Have you ever wondered where the animals come from that you see caged in pet stores?

This book is about a tiny dog named Mimi who lived in fear for the first 4-½ years of her life. It is a story of a rescue from a puppy mill and a new life she learned to live by overcoming her fears. It is Mimi herself telling you that you CAN overcome your fears when you have the love and support of your friends and family to help you.

Fear does not have control of your life once you learn that YOU can be strong and have the courage to conquer what challenges you will face in your life. Mimi tells how she came to her loving forever home and the adventures she faced on her road to recovery and happiness. It is the story about the friends she meets along the way and how she learns that even though she is small in size, she can help others in a big way.

Mimi learns through both human and animal friends - dogs, cats, and even a pig named Trixie – that knowledge is power. Knowing what goes on behind what the general public sees, finding out how you can change things, sharing your knowledge to help others – those are signs of a successful transformation from a scared little trapped puppy, to the Mighty Mimi she has become.

Who knows what adventures and experiences Mimi will face beyond the pages of this book. Whatever they are, she will strongly face them with her newly found courage, friends and family by her side.

Contributed by
Aurora Golden-Appleton, Age 7

PROBLEM

People don't know what's going on therefore they can't do anything about it and it will go on forever.

LEARN MORE

Google™ "Pet store cruelty" and "pet free" pet stores. They treat them horribly and put them in the back room to die without any vet care. Even though you don't see it doesn't mean its not there.

HELP

- Buy PET SUPPLIES ONLY at animal free pet stores (stores that do not sell dogs or cats, as well as guinea pigs, gerbils, chinchillas, birds, fish, and other small animals). You not only help animals big and small but you'll feel better too because the more small things you do the more you help!
- Raise money for a humane society.
- Volunteer at a local animal shelter.

This 'unedited' article is included in this book because it shows that even children can care about the abuse that animals suffer in puppy mills.

This was my life for over 4 years.

Mighty Mimi...

That seems like a strange title for such a little girl like me. How can I be mighty when I only weighed 6 pounds when I was adopted by my new family? I had been living in a puppy mill the first 4½ years of my life and never saw life outside of my cage. I had one litter of puppies after another. The puppies stayed with me a little while, then they were sold and the cycle started again. There was no human warmth or affection. No one cuddled me or gave me comfort when I hurt. It was such a sad time for me.

When the rescue group came and got several of us from the puppy mill, I was so scared. I had never been around people and was afraid they would hurt me. I went to a foster family who had several children. There were many other dogs there in the family's home, in various stages of being adopted out to their forever homes. I mostly huddled in my little area of the house, afraid to even venture outside. After all, I did not know what that green stuff was under my feet or if it would hurt me. I had never seen grass before, or sunshine, or felt the warmth of a summer breeze on my face.

Who wouldn't want this lovable face?

I'd been living at the foster home for several weeks when a family from Columbus Ohio saw my face on the internet ad that was placed for my adoption.

The Mom of that family loved dogs. She saw my face and read my story about how scared I was. She knew that she had to come get me. She felt that she could help me as she had helped several other dogs in her life. Happily, she proved to be right. But that is a long story so I better get started telling you how it went.

Mom Louise, as I came to know her name, drove 250 miles to come get me to join her family. I met her at my foster house and I thought at once that she seemed like a kind person. I let her hold me. She held me very gently, and it felt good to be in her arms. I could barely walk because my back legs were so weak from being kept in a cage all my life and never getting any exercise.

That was a long ride home. I huddled next to her in the car but could not fall asleep because I was shaking from fear of the unknown. So much had happened to me in such a short time. I was rescued out of the puppy mill, taken to a vet to be spayed so I would not be forced to have more puppies, and given a bath. I was in shock. My hair was matted from not being groomed but the bath helped me at least feel cleaner. Now, somehow deep inside I knew things would get better.

I do feel much cleaner
and warmly welcomed.

When we reached my new Mom's house, I was greeted by five creatures that would later become my best friends and adopted sisters. Frisbee and Frazier were Bichon Frise puppy mill rescues like I was. Rosie was a Yorkie-Poo rescue from an abandoned house. Indy and Rainbow were cat rescues with stories of their own. Rainbow was found hundreds of miles from Columbus in a warehouse in Kentucky and Indy was just dropped off at a vet's office near my new Mom's home. They all greeted me with wagging tails and welcoming grins to say *"Hello! We are glad you are here.   This is a safe and happy place."*

So my new life started. I spent most of my time huddled underneath the bed. I would only come out to eat when no one was looking and I ran away from Mom anytime she tried to come near me. But she had such wisdom to let me run like I did. In all my running away from her up and down the hall, my back legs gained strength every day. All four of us dogs went to what they call a "groomer" and I got another bath and my first haircut. The ladies there were so gentle and kind. When they were finished with me, I felt really clean and even pretty.

These beds are comfortable and I can
leave this open cage anytime I want.

After a few months I was running away from Mom at a slower speed. She did not seem to want to hurt me. Mom had little beds in every room for me to cuddle in. Pretty soon I was in the bed in the living room near all my other sisters more than the one in the back bedroom. There were open cages that we could go in and out of if we felt the need for some extra security and they all had comfortable beds in them as well.

I kept watching Frasier and Frisbee and Rosie and how they acted. They would jump on Mom's lap whenever she sat down. They would lick her hands and face. *"They must really like her,"* I thought to myself. Little did I know then that they really loved Mom and for good reasons, as I was to learn.

Mom cooked special food for all of us because Rosie and Frisbee were allergic to normal dog food. So we all ate the special food mixed with cooked and shredded chicken and it was really good. I had a special dish of my own in the back bedroom because I was still afraid to eat with everyone else. Mom never complained about having to walk extra steps to fill my dish and she always stepped out of the room so she would not see me eat. She understood that I could not eat with anyone watching. She seemed so understanding about all my fears.

When the weather turned warm I started to wonder about the backyard. I could not climb stairs but I was getting more comfortable with Mom. I was letting her walk up to me and pick me up now. She would pick me up ever so gently and take me down the deck steps to the huge backyard. It was so strange. At first I just huddled along the fence. Since all I had known all my life was walls, the fence felt safer.

I just feel safer here under the fence.

I watched all my sisters run and play in the grass. They seemed so comfortable. Soon I started slowly making my way out into the yard. The grass was warm and soft under my feet. It felt good.

This grass feels good!

I knew I could, I knew I could!

I know I can, I know I can...

I think I can, I think I can...

But Mom always had to carry me back up the deck steps. They were like a huge mountain that I could never climb.

One day we were all out in the backyard playing. Mom's granddaughter Reece had come to visit and stay overnight. I was not afraid of her mainly because she was not as tall as Mom. I thought the smaller the person the safer they would be.

When everyone else just ran up the steps, I decided to give it a try. I took first one step, then another. My legs had gotten so strong that they could now actually push me up the steps. I made it all the way to the top.

Mom started looking for me in the yard to carry me back up. She asked Reece if she had seen me anywhere. Reece said, "Look up here Grandma!" The look on her face when she saw me at the top on the deck was priceless. She was so happy – for me – happy that I had conquered another fear.

Fear will not control me!
I can do this!

But several days later I started up and fell down two steps. Mom caught me right away but it scared me really badly. I was afraid all over again to try the steps but Mom never complained about carrying me up.

All creatures experience fears at some point in their lives. But I discovered that I had found a safe home where I could work to overcome my fears. My pace was slow but I was determined to get better. One beautiful spring day we were all out in the yard. I stood at the bottom of the steps I had previously conquered, wanting to join my friends back up on the deck. I was afraid. If I climbed, would I fall again like I did last time?

But Frazier, Frisbee, Rosie and my Mom were all up on the deck already. Mom was encouraging me. "You can do it Mimi, I know you can," she called from the top of the steps. Frazier and Frisbee came to the edge of the deck. "*Come on Mimi, you can do this. We believe in you,*" they barked over and over again. So I started up those 13 steps and wouldn't you know it? I made it all the way up!

"*We are so proud of you Mimi!*" they all chimed in when I reached the top. "*We knew you could do it!*" They believed in me and that was what gave me the courage to try those steps again. When people - and your fellow dogs - believe in you and encourage you to succeed, it gives you the strength to try what seems like some impossible task.

Running with the pack.

Hurry up, Mom! I smell trouble!

Now I climb the deck steps whenever it is time to go back into the house. When everyone runs outside I run out with them. I used to cower in the living room and Mom would have to get behind me and kind of nudge me to go outside, but now if I need to go out I run out with the others. At first I was afraid to run past Mom when I came into the house but now I run in with everyone else.

But the inside steps are harder because they are smoother and not carpeted. I have not mastered them yet. When Mom and the gang are downstairs in the house working I stay up in the living room. That proved to be a real lifesaver (and home-saver) one day.

Mom had started to heat some soup on the stove. Then for some reason she went back downstairs and forgot the soup. It started to overheat and burn. I started barking over and over like crazy to call Mom. She had never heard me bark like that before and instantly recognized that something was different. "That's Mimi barking," she said to Frazier. "What is going on?"

The smoke detectors had not even gone off yet but I was able to smell trouble. Even Frisbee and Frazier were not warning Mom. Mom came rushing upstairs and smelled the problem when she reached the top step. She rushed the pan outside and prevented it from catching the cabinets on fire. "You saved our house Mimi, you are a hero!" Mom said. She told all her friends how brave I was to warn her like I did.

I weigh a
whopping
9 pounds now!

I'll just watch.

By now I had been living with Mom and my adopted sisters for over a year. I weighed a whopping 9 pounds thanks to all that good food. Mom can now come up to me and pick me up and I do not run away from her. I like to sit on her lap and can even fall asleep since I am so comfortable there. Frisbee washes my face all the time and Rosie and Frazier are trying to teach me how to play with toys. I never learned to play before so I am slow to catch on to that fun but I like to watch them play tug-of-war with each other. Sometimes Frazier, Rosie and Frisbee all grab the same toy and tug in all different directions. It is so funny! My fears are going away because I am surrounded by people and friends who love and support me.

I have even reached a point now where I can eat my food when someone is watching. Reece came to stay again one weekend and was holding me in her lap while watching TV. She set my food dish down next to me in the chair and I just started eating. I was hungry and it just seemed like the right thing to do. I had never before eaten in front of anyone. It was another victory over fear. Mom was really happy for me, like she was every time I made progress.

Yes, this IS the way dogs say hello.

I prefer nose to nose myself.

One day Mom took me to visit a friend of hers who had a dog that wanted to meet me. I was surprised when we got there by how big he was. Simba was his name and he and I got along great. You would think I would have been afraid of such a big dog, but when Simba first said hello to me I knew he would not hurt me. We walked all around his yard and had a great visit. We explored the yard together for several hours.

Safety first!

I go to the dog park now with my sisters, meet new friends when Mom goes to visit her human friends and I am beginning to feel like a real dog.

There is one special visit I could hardly wait to tell my sisters about. Mom has a friend who lives on a farm. Mom took only me to visit the farm. Wow, what an experience that was! I was a little nervous because I did not know where we were going or why I had to ride so far to get there. I was put in a carrier that Mom fastened to the seat with the seat belt for safety.

I know why she put me in the carrier. Once Mom was in a car accident and the seat belt that she fastened around herself on that short trip saved her from really serious injury. Sure she got bruised and sore from the seat belt and will have some recovery time from the accident's bruises, but that seat belt saved her life so she could continue to take care of me and my sisters. If you are reading this to your pet, you need to explain to them why they need to be fastened with a seat belt when they ride in the car with you and not sit on your lap.

On the way to the farm, we stopped at a rest stop so I could go potty and Mom put this thing called a leash on me. At first I hardly moved but after a few minutes it did not seem so strange so I started walking around. This was my first exposure with a leash.

Buttons and Spurs say hello at the farm.

Dan primping in the bathtub.

When we got to the farm Mom's friend, Barb, seemed so nice that she did not scare me. Mom told Barb that Mom and I needed some one-on-one time.

We all went out to the barn and I met some really interesting friends. There was Kiss the pinto horse, Fred and even Bo all came in from the pasture to say hello. The horses blew on me with their noses and it tickled but I was not scared. They were so big compared to little me but they seemed gentle. I met Spurs the Blue Healer dog, Buttons the miniature Schnauzer, Gabby the Siamese cat, and Dan, the cat who seemed to own the barn and the house in his opinion.

Even big horses don't scare me now!

Cowboy even came to visit when I was there. He was a rescue dog of unknown type from a truck stop and he and his owner came to help out on the farm. Mom held me in her arms when I was meeting everyone and they all talked to me and I was not scared at all.

Then we went to visit the farm of Barb's daughter and granddaughter. There I met some miniature horses named Charlie and Miriah. They were much smaller than Bo and Fred and Kiss and were the perfect size for little Alyssa to ride as she was only two years old. I met their Blue Healer dog named Gator, the Puggle named Peanut Butter and even a goat named Billy Goat. I saw chickens and cows too. There were two draft ponies there named Dot and Dutch. They were some kind of breed named Halflingers I heard Barb tell my Mom.

Then we went to visit Barb's Mom in the small city near their farms and met a very curious cat named Furby. He kept coming up to me to sniff my nose. The whole time I was there, thanks to all the previous help from Mom and my sisters, I was not afraid at all. All the animals were friendly to me and they all said how glad they were to meet me.

Life is good!

I still have some underlying fears but Mom and the gang at home are always there to encourage and help me. Now whenever Mom comes home there are four happy barking dogs greeting her at the top of the steps. Fear only controls you if you let it. Don't give up on your friend or your pet if it takes them a long time to achieve a specific goal. It took my sister Frisbee a year to learn to go potty outside. It took my sister Frazier 6 months to learn to take her allergy medicine. She finally learned that it would help her feel better. My bad memories are fading away and I hope my story will encourage you to rescue a frightened or lonely animal someday.

It seems I am destined to
have very large friends!

By the way, in mentioning overcoming fear, yes, you guessed it! I have conquered the indoor steps! I amazed Mom one day. She was carrying something up the steps while trying to carry me too. We got to the first landing and Mom put me down to take her bundle up to the top steps. She turned around to come back down the steps to get me and I was right beside her. Boy was she surprised. Who knows what I will accomplish next?

Also, there is one more accomplishment I need to share with you. I found out that I was not the only one who had fears. Mom worked with a lady whose dog Bailey was getting old and had really bad hips. The Busse family tried building him a ramp to help him get out to the backyard but he was afraid of the ramp. So Mom decided to take me to visit him, and I am really glad she did. I had learned so much from my family, now it was time for me to share all that knowledge with someone else. Little did I know how much help I would be.

When we pulled into their yard, we went into the backyard and there I met Bailey.

Don't be sad, fear is a real thing!

One step at a time, see how I do it?

Bailey was 10 years old and his hips were really giving him problems. I told him about a friend of mine that I met at the dog park named Duffy. He was in his spirit body when I met him but he had lived the last three years of his earthly life in a special wheel chair made by a company at *www.enablingpets.com*. The owner, a very special man named Richard, makes special carts for dogs with leg problems. I was telling Bailey about Duffy's story when my Mom was telling the Busse family the same thing. They decided right then and there that they were going to contact that company to get Bailey some help.

Bailey was sad. *"I know my family is trying to help me,"* he said, *"but that ramp just scares me. I am sad that I am disappointing my family and making it harder on them to have to carry my big body up and down. I used to be the protective one when Deven was a baby and now he has to protect and watch over me."* I could see the sadness in his eyes.

So I decided I had to help Bailey. I led him over to the ramp and told him about how much I had been afraid of the steps and that now I had a good time running up those very steps that used to scare me.

I told Bailey that the ramp would help him get up and down and not hurt his legs as badly as steps would hurt. He stood there for the longest time. *"How do I know that? It seems so steep,"* he said in his very deep voice.

See? Just lift your paw and take a step.

Time for a well deserved rest.

"*You have to trust me,*" I said. "*I know how you feel because I felt the same way about the steps at my house. But you can do this, you really can.*" It took several minutes of me just telling Bailey he could do it when he decided to give it a try. Being such a gentle giant of a dog it probably seems strange that a thing like this would scare him, but fears are real, no matter what your size or how they originate.

I shouted as loudly as my little voice could shout. I was so pleased when Bailey reached the top of the deck and sat down to rest. I was so grateful to my family that they had the patience to teach me how to overcome my fears, too. Now I could share that conquest with others so they could know that fear need not control their lives. No matter how big or small you are, fears seem like huge mountains that can never be climbed, wide rivers that can never be crossed, but now we know that is not true.

There is another learning lesson that I need to share with you from my experience with Bailey. Remember when I told Bailey, *"You need to trust me"*? Well, trust is something that most of us rescue animals do not have. When I first went to my Mom's house, I would not let her hold me. I would not even run past her. Why do you think that is? It is because I did not trust her. Humans had been mistreating me for over the first four years of my life and I had no idea what this new human in my life would do. I didn't know if she would hurt me in some way.

As I came to know both my dog sisters and my new Mom, I developed a very calm feeling around them. I noticed that I did not get quite so scared when they approached me.

I told Mimi she can do anything!

"Hey, this isn't as hard as I thought!"

One time when Mom had to go out of town my sisters and I went to what is called a boarding place. This place is run by a very kind lady named Rebecca and she even helped me to surprise Mom when she got home. Rebecca is also what they call a dog trainer. She decided it was time for me to learn how to go down steps since Mom told her I could now climb up the steps. She very patiently worked with me and – you guessed it – yes, I can now go UP and DOWN steps.

I can even run to greet Mom when she comes home now along with all my other sisters. At first I always held back because I was afraid if being in "the crowd". But I learned that we were all just glad to see her and she made space for petting all of us. Now I just crowd in there with all my sisters for my hello pats and I know that no one will hurt me or bite me or push me aside deliberately. I am beginning to trust my sisters and know that we are all being watched over with all the love that Mom has to give.

I even started sleeping at the foot of Mom's bed instead of in my safe little cuddle bed on the floor. Mom at first put my whole cuddle bed at the foot of her bed so I would feel more secure, then one day just set me on the bed itself to sleep for the night. I really surprised her one morning. She would usually say, "Good morning, girls," when she woke up each day. Immediately Frisbee, Frazier, and Rosie would rush over from their appointed spots on the bed to lick her hands and face to say good morning themselves. One morning she felt this really small head nudging her hands and licking them. "That's Mimi," she exclaimed to the rest of my sisters. Mom was really surprised and even I was surprised that I could now do that just like my sisters. I do it every morning now and even sometimes cuddle up right next to her when she rubs my head.

Mimi asks Rosie, Frisbee, Frazier, Indy
and Rainbow:
*"So, where do you think Mom will
sleep tonight?"*

I guess that is also part of that feeling of trust that I was missing all my life. I can look at Mom now when she holds me and picks me up and I don't have a scared look on my face. Mom says she can see in my eyes that I am not as afraid any longer.

I even got to be a part of a school presentation with all my new-found confidence. My Mom and I got to do the presentation for a school to help the students learn how to take better care of their animals and to make sure they spayed and neutered them.

That was a really awesome experience. A little girl named Aurora did a book report about my life story to tell her classmates how bad conditions are in puppy mills and what they could do to stop the abuse animals that are trapped there suffer.

Aurora wrote the article in the front of this book and was only seven years old at the time she wrote it. She really loves animals and is doing all she can to help make life better for as many as she and her family can help.

"You and me, Mimi, we can tell them what it was like for you."

"Don't be scared. Mom and I will be there with you."

After Aurora and her sister Kylie finished the report to the class, Mom and I came out from around the corner to surprise everyone by introducing them to the 'star' of the book. Imagine me being petted by 40 excited children who got to meet me. I was so honored to help play a part in educating children about what I had suffered in that puppy mill from which I was rescued. I wasn't even scared because I knew deep down inside that Mom would not take me anywhere that would cause me any harm. That is the trust that has been building inside of me over the time I have been with Mom and my sisters. We are planning on doing the same presentation to other schools in our area to educate and inform people about how they can help improve the lives of those still trapped in those puppy mills.

"You, too, can prevent animal abuse,"
say Kylie and Aurora.

You can be a foster family as well as we can.

I also now have met some new friends named Balto and Gigi. They are the dogs who live with Aurora and her family. They help foster animals for the Ohio Puppy Rescue organization. I call them "professional fosterers" because they have helped so many dogs in the past and will probably help many others in the future.

I spent some time with their foster puppies in their pen. I told them they didn't have to be afraid. They would be going to new homes where they would be loved and appreciated.

"Don't be afraid, you'll go to good homes soon."

Some of the other new friends I have met recently are a little more on what I would call the strange side. Mom took me to a farm in Grove City to meet the star of another book called "There's a Pot On My Belly". The star of that book is a pot-belly pig named Trixie. What a strange encounter that was. I have to admit I was a little scared, but Trixie was really kind.

That IS one strange looking dog!

One of Trixie's brothers was a dog named Brutus. That dog was really, really big. But like Trixie, he was gentle and kind and meant me no harm. It sure is interesting not knowing where Mom will take me next or what new adventures lie in store for my sisters and I.

Can a face that looks this kind have a mean bone anywhere in his body?

Time is passing and I had an even stranger event in my life recently. I was getting ready to run outside with my sisters when we got up one morning. Mom opened the door, I ran out, and *"Whoa! What happened to that warm green grass under my feet?"* There was this cold white stuff on the deck and all over the grass. Mom called it snow!

"What is this stuff? It's COLD!!!!"

Needless to say, none of us stayed outside very long. Mom did explain that it is a short-lived problem that goes away every spring. Thank goodness for that.

"This is not that nice warm green grass under my feet that I am used to feeling!"

I hope you have learned from my story that the sky's the limit when it comes to stopping fear in its tracks. Trust is something that comes slowly to rescue animals, but with patience and love, it does come. I hope my story will help you to understand that fear does not have to consume your life but that you can overcome past hardships and sorrows when you have people and friends who encourage and support you to be the best that you can be. Now I can help and support others myself. I can help to rescue other trapped animals by educating people about the conditions that exist. I now truly feel like a Mighty Mimi.

Mimi gets a well deserved rest.

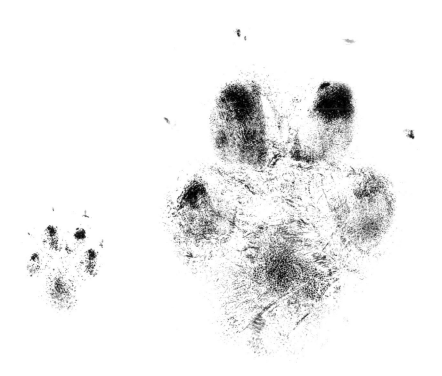

Mimi and Bailey
give their stamp of approval
to this book.

Made in the USA
Charleston, SC
07 January 2012